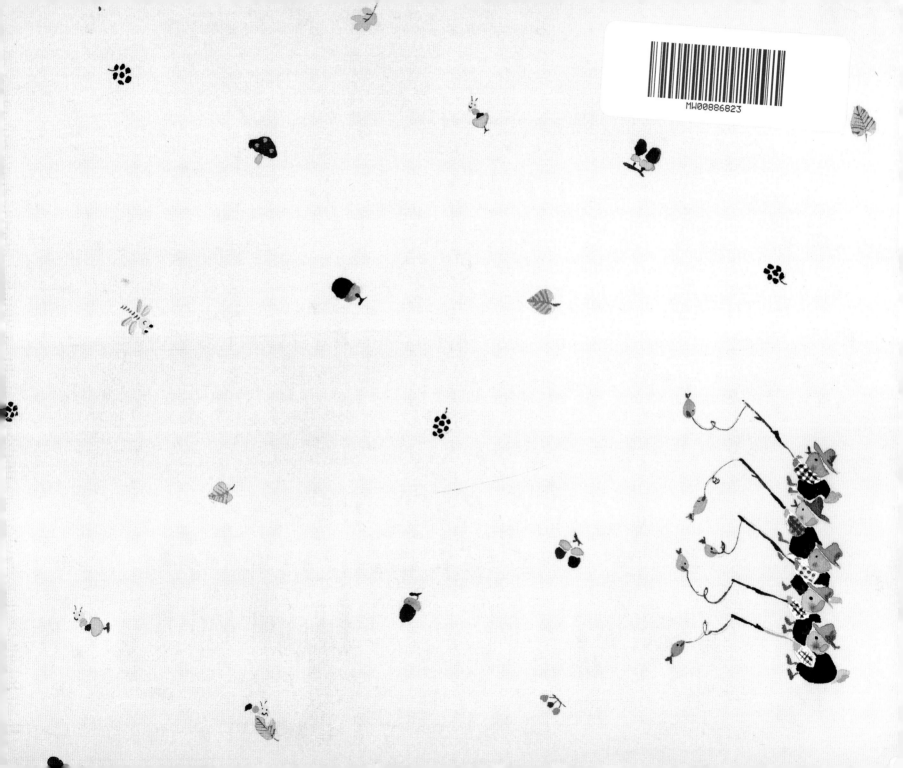

MW00886823

For my family—L. B.

For Koharu—H. N.

Henry Holt and Company, LLC, *Publishers since 1866*
175 Fifth Avenue, New York, New York 10010
www.HenryHoltKids.com

Henry Holt® is a registered trademark of Henry Holt and Company, LLC.
Text copyright © 2009 by Lynne Berry
Illustrations copyright © 2009 by Hiroe Nakata
All rights reserved.
Distributed in Canada by H. B. Fenn and Company Ltd.

Library of Congress Cataloging-in-Publication Data
Berry, Lynne.
Duck tents / Lynne Berry ; illustrated by Hiroe Nakata.—1st ed.
p.   cm.
Summary: While on a camping trip, five little ducks pitch tents, go fishing,
toast marshmallows around a campfire, and face frightening night noises.
ISBN-13: 978-0-8050-8696-6 / ISBN-10: 0-8050-8696-X
[1. Stories in rhyme. 2. Camping—Fiction. 3. Ducks—Fiction.]
I. Nakata, Hiroe, ill. II. Title.
PZ8.3.B4593Duk 2009   [E]—dc22   2008013376

First Edition—2009
The artist used watercolor and ink to create the illustrations for this book.
Printed in China on acid-free paper. ∞
1 3 5 7 9 10 8 6 4 2

Duck Tents

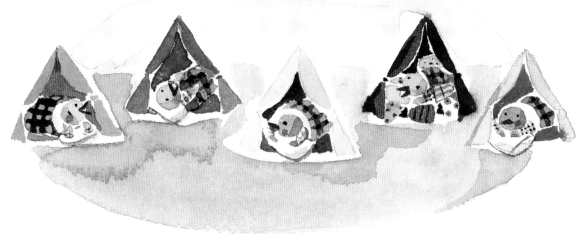

Lynne Berry

ILLUSTRATED BY Hiroe Nakata

HENRY HOLT AND COMPANY 🍄 NEW YORK

HERRICK DISTRICT LIBRARY
300 S. River Avenue
Holland, MI 49423

MAY 2 o 2009

In a small backyard, by a squat stone fence,
Five little ducks pitch five duck tents.

"All five up!" five proud ducks cheer.
Ducks fill tents with camping gear:

Lanterns, pillows, sleeping bags,
Fishing poles—brand-new with tags.

Five little ducks each grab one pole.
"Hurry, ducks! To the fishing hole!"

Five little ducks in five straw hats

Tramp through the woods with chairs and mats.

Ducks dig worms. Ducks bait hooks.

Ducks flop down with snacks and books—

To wait and wait and wait and wait—
Is that a tug on one duck's bait?

One duck yanks.

Two ducks lunge.

Three ducks lean.

Four ducks plunge.

Five ducks heave and five ducks haul.

One duck slips—and four ducks sprawl!

The pole goes *zoom*. The fish leaps high.
"We lost the big one!" five ducks cry.

Shadows stretch through the moss-covered glade.
Damp ducks shake in the cool of the shade.
"Time for a campfire!" two ducks quack.
"Come on, ducks! Let's all head back."

Four little ducks reel in four lines.

Five ducks tramp through the oaks and pines.

Campfire flames burn down to coals—
Ducks toast marshmallows on their poles!
Outside crispy, inside sticky,
Chewy, gooey, finger-licky.

Five ducks sigh, full of marshmallow goo.
Five little ducks hear a *whoo-whoo-whooooooo*.

Ducks all dive for their tents in a row,

Zip up tight, and lie down low.

Two little ducks poke out two beaks.

"I'm not scared," one little duck squeaks.

"I'm not scared," quack two, three, four.

The fifth little duck pretends to snore.

Yet five little ducks can't help but hear
Sounds of the nighttime, loud and clear.

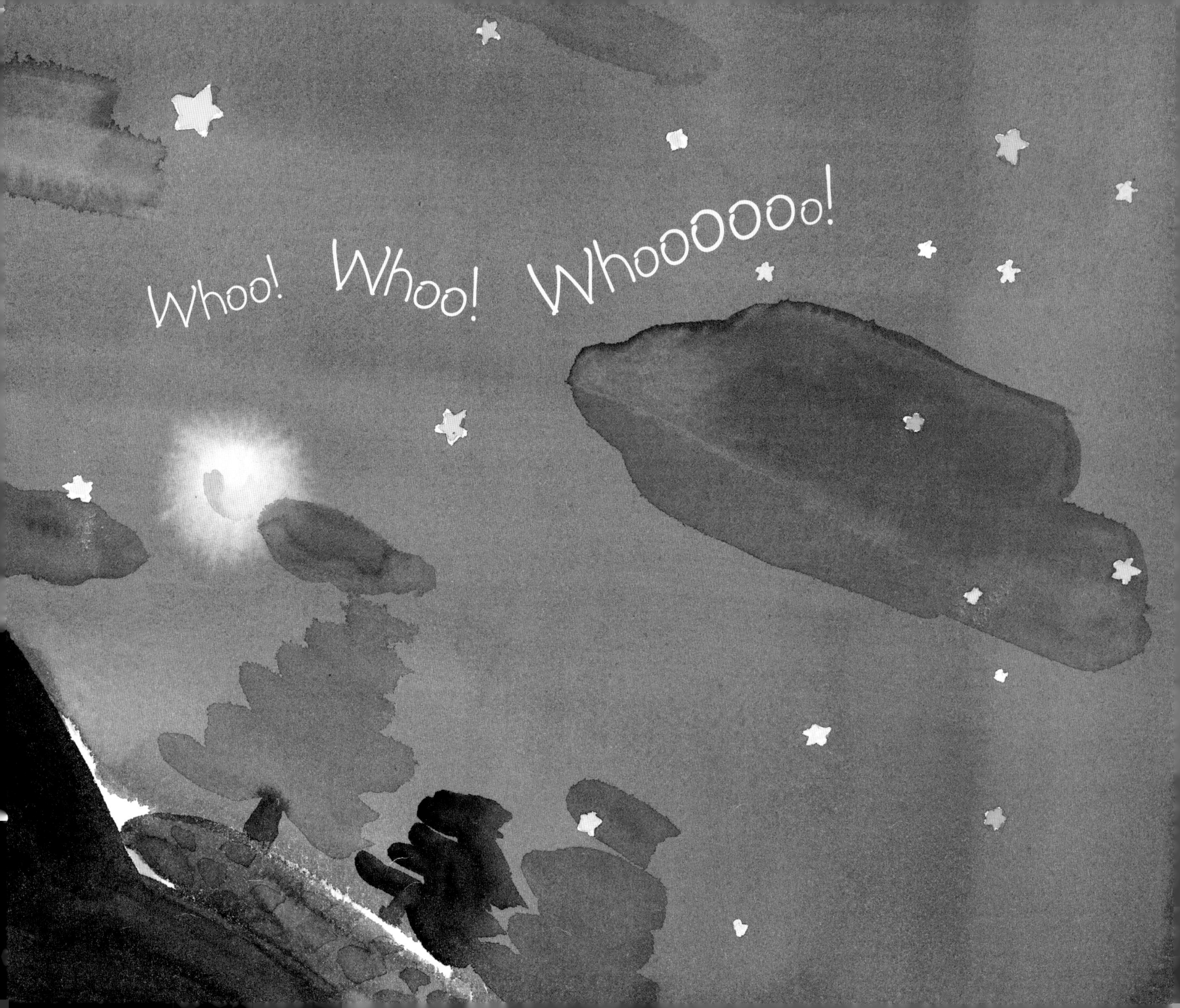

Whoo! Whoo! WhooOOOo!

One by one, four little ducks creep . . .
"Not scared *now*," ducks sigh and peep,
And snuggle up tight and drift to sleep.

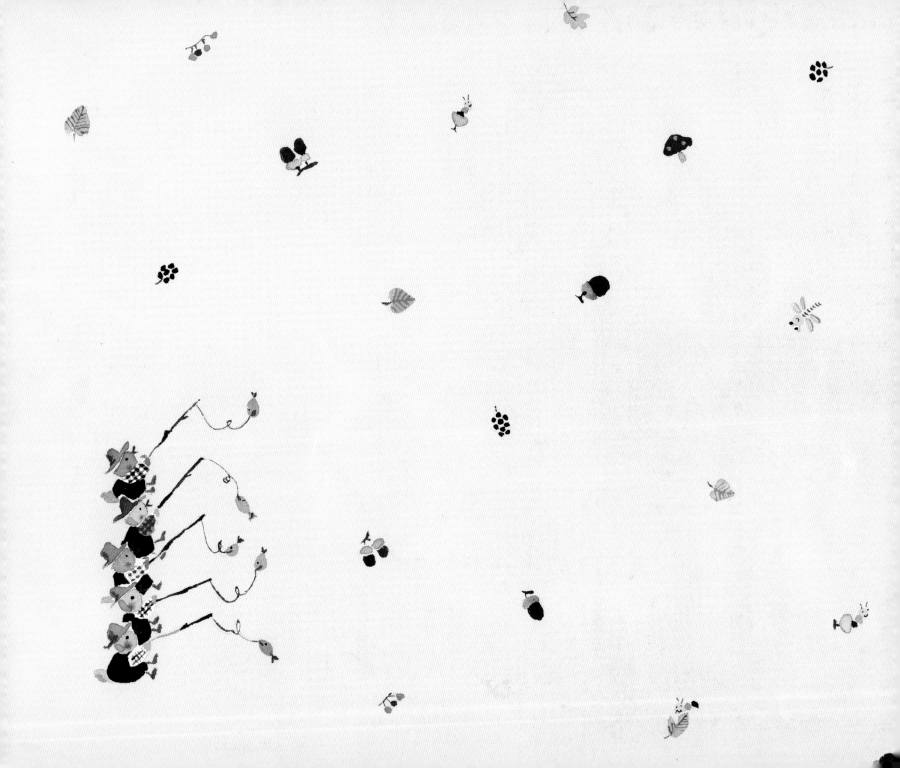